Paloma the Dodgems Fairy

Join the **Rainbow Magic Reading Challenge!**

Read the story and collect your fairy points to climb the
r   Rainbow at the back of the book.

ORCHARD BOOKS

First published in Great Britain in 2018 by The Watts Publishing Group

1 3 5 7 9 10 8 6 4 2

© 2018 Rainbow Magic Limited.
© 2018 HIT Entertainment Limited.
Illustrations © Orchard Books 2018

HIT entertainment

A CIP catalogue record for this book is available from the British Library.

ISBN 978 1 40834 961 8

Printed and bound in Great Britain by CPI Group (UK) Ltd, Croydon, CR0 4YY

MIX
Paper from
responsible sources
FSC
www.fsc.org
FSC® C104740

The paper and board used in this book are made from wood from responsible sources

Orchard Books
An imprint of Hachette Children's Group
Part of The Watts Publishing Group Limited
Carmelite House, 50 Victoria Embankment, London EC4Y 0DZ

An Hachette UK Company
www.hachette.co.uk
www.hachettechildrens.co.uk

Paloma
the Dodgems
Fairy

by Daisy Meadows

ORCHARD

www.rainbowmagic.co.uk

The Fairyland Palace

Fairyland Funfair

Rachel's House

TIPPINGTON TOWN

Jack Frost's Spell

I want a funfair just for me!
(I'll let in goblins, grudgingly.)
With stolen keyrings in my hand,
I'll spoil the fun the fairies planned.

Their rides will stop, their stalls will fail,
Their food will all turn sour and stale.
I'll make the goblins squeal and smirk.
This time my plan is going to work!

Contents

A Hidden Fairy

"I wish The Fernandos' Fabulous Funfair could stay on my school playing field for ever," said Rachel Walker as she skipped along. "I had a brilliant time yesterday, and there's still so much more to do."

"Can you imagine having a funfair at school?" said her best friend, Kirsty Tate. "No one would get any lessons done."

"And we wouldn't want to leave at home time," Rachel added with a giggle.

The sun was shining, and the girls were looking forward to another exciting day at the funfair. Kirsty was staying with Rachel all weekend, and they were planning to spend every possible moment enjoying the funfair. Up ahead, they could see two girls leaning over the wooden entrance gate and waving at them.

"Morning, Matilda!" called Rachel. "Hi, Georgia!"

Matilda and Georgia Fernando were twin sisters, and their parents ran the funfair. Rachel and Kirsty had met them the day before, and the four girls had made friends straight away.

"Good morning," said Matilda,

grinning at them. "I'm glad you're here so early – we've got so much to show you! What do you want to try first?"

"What would you choose?" Kirsty asked.

"How about the dodgems?" said

Georgia, her eyes sparkling. "They're always fun."

"Oh yes, I love dodgems," said Rachel.

They bought their tickets from the little booth that stood just inside the gate. Today, the tickets were ruby red with a rainbow-coloured trim.

"These tickets are even more beautiful than yesterday's purple ones," said Kirsty.

"We sell a different coloured ticket every day," said Matilda. "We go through all the colours of the rainbow."

Rachel and Kirsty exchanged a

secret smile as they all ran into the
playing field. Talking of rainbows always
reminded them of the first fairies they
had ever met, the Rainbow Fairies. Since
then they had shared many adventures
with the fairies.

"This way to the dodgems," called
Matilda.

She and her sister led Rachel and

Kirsty over to the red-and-gold dodgem rink. Coloured lights were flashing and summery songs were blasting out. Even though it was early, there were already a few children in the cars.

The operator was a young woman with short brown hair.

"Hi, Becky," called Matilda, waving to her.

Becky waved back. Matilda and Georgia jumped into a pink car together, and Rachel and Kirsty chose a red one.

"The other cars are filling up fast," said Rachel, looking around.

Soon, children were squealing and giggling in every single car.

"Have fun!" Becky called out.

She pressed the button to make the cars work, but nothing happened. Becky

pressed the button again. This time, the
dodgem cars began to spin around and
around on the spot.

"Hey, what's going wrong?" one boy
cried out.

"This is more like spinning teacups than dodgems," said Rachel.

"Becky, this is making me feel ill," said Georgia.

Becky pressed the button again, and the cars stopped spinning. The lights faded, and the cheerful music was suddenly cut off.

"I'm sorry," she said. "I don't know what's wrong. You will 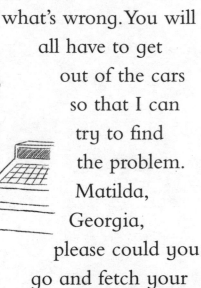 all have to get out of the cars so that I can try to find the problem. Matilda, Georgia, please could you go and fetch your parents? I'm going to need their help."

Matilda and Georgia hurried off at once, and Kirsty and Rachel started to climb out of their dodgem car.

"Wait," said Kirsty, putting her hand on Rachel's arm. "Look down there, under the steering wheel."

Rachel smiled when she saw a golden glow below the steering wheel. She knew

exactly what it meant. There must be
magic close by. The girls bent down as
if they had dropped something, and saw
Paloma the Dodgems Fairy in the foot
space.

"Kirsty, Rachel," she said in a whisper.
"I've come to ask for your help."

Dodgems on the Loose

Paloma was wearing a dungaree dress and a crisp white T-shirt, and her dark-blonde hair was swishing around her shoulders under her black hat. Behind her black-rimmed glasses, her eyes looked worried.

"Paloma, it's good to see you," whispered Rachel. "You've come just at the right moment. The dodgems aren't

working."

"I know," said Paloma, her eyes brimming with tears. "I must find my magical key ring and put everything right. Without it, I can't make sure that dodgems are lots of fun."

Rachel and Kirsty exchanged a glance. Fairies were usually so kind and happy that it was horrible to see one of them looking so upset.

"We'll do whatever we can to help you find your key ring," said Kirsty.

"We won't let you and the other Funfair Fairies down."

Her mind raced back over all the adventures they had shared in the last twenty-four hours. Almost as soon as the girls had arrived at the funfair the day before, they had met Rae the Rollercoaster Fairy. She had whisked them to Fairyland and introduced them to the rest of the Funfair Fairies – Fatima the Face-Painting Fairy, Paloma the Dodgems Fairy and Bobbi the Bouncy Castle Fairy.

"Thank you for being such good friends to us," said Paloma. "We all know that we can count on your help to get our key rings back soon – before the Fairyland Summer Fair and the funfair here in Tippington are both ruined."

The Funfair Fairies and the queen and king of Fairyland had planned a grand Summer Fair in the grounds of the Fairyland Palace. But Jack Frost and his goblins had stolen the Funfair Fairies' magical key rings. Jack Frost was planning to build a funfair in the middle of his castle. Without the key rings, no one but Jack Frost and the goblins would be able to enjoy funfair games and rides. Rachel and Kirsty had helped two of the Funfair Fairies to get their magical key rings back, but there were still two key rings left to find. Time was running out, because the Fairyland funfair was opening that evening.

"Hide in here," said Rachel, holding open her pocket. "We have to get off the dodgem rink so that Becky and the

Fernandos can try to mend it."

Paloma fluttered into Rachel's pocket, and then the best friends stepped out of the dodgem car and walked off the rink. Kirsty glanced back, hoping that they would see the dodgems working again soon. To her surprise, she saw that there were still two children sitting in a dodgem car.

"Hang on a moment," she said to

Rachel. "I wonder why those children haven't moved. Maybe they didn't hear Becky ask us all to leave the rink. Should we go back and tell them?"

Rachel didn't have a chance to reply. Suddenly, the children's dodgem car started to zoom forwards. It bumped the other cars out of the way, getting faster

and faster. Green sparks flew from the flag. Then it flew off the rink, over the heads of the girls and on to the playing field.

People gasped and pointed as the dodgem car trundled past them.

"A runaway dodgem!" they shouted.

"Oh my goodness!" said Rachel.

"Surely dodgems shouldn't be able to work outside the rink?"

Kirsty nodded, looking confused. Then suddenly her eyes widened.

"Rachel, I just saw something that might explain how the dodgem got off the rink," she said. "I think that the people inside had green faces!"

Rachel gasped. "That explains why the children didn't do as they were told and get out of the car. They're not children at all. They're goblins!"

Dangerous Drivers

"Goblins or not, how did they manage to get the dodgem car off the rink?" Kirsty asked.

"Good question," said Paloma from inside Rachel's pocket. "Dodgem cars should only be able to work on the rink. They are goblins, and they must have my magical key ring."

"Then we have to follow them," said Kirsty at once. "Quickly, let's find a place to hide so that Paloma can turn us into fairies."

Quickly, the girls ducked down behind the golden-and-red railing of the dodgem rink. Paloma fluttered out of Rachel's pocket. She traced two tiny circles in

the air with the tip of her wand, and
each circle turned into a shining bubble.
The bubbles floated down to land on
Rachel and Kirsty. As soon as the bubbles
touched the girls, they popped. Silver
fairy dust was sprinkled all over them,
and they instantly shrank to fairy size.
Gauzy wings fluttered on their backs.

"Here we go!" Rachel cried out,
twirling as she zoomed upwards.

Paloma and Kirsty were close behind
her. High above the crowds of people,
they flew after the dodgem car. It was
bumping across the playing field, and
everyone was pointing at it.

"Faster!" Kirsty called out, darting
ahead. "I can see them, and they're
definitely goblins."

There were two goblins crammed

into the car. One was hunched over the steering wheel, his long nose skimming the front of the car. The other was enjoying the ride with his enormous feet up on the dashboard, his arms folded. He was wearing a pair of goggles to protect

his eyes from the wind.

"We have to get closer," said Rachel, diving downwards.

"But what if we're seen?" asked Paloma
in a worried voice.

"No one's looking at us," said Rachel
over her shoulder. "They're all turning
away from the car, they're not watching
who's following it."

The fairies flew faster and faster,

their wings a hazy blur. They were
close enough now to hear the goblins
squabbling.

"My turn to drive," said the goblin with
his feet up.

He jabbed his elbows into the driver goblin, who let out a squawk and jabbed him back.

"I've hardly had any time at all," he wailed. "Leave me alone."

They tussled over the steering wheel, and the dodgem car swerved. The second goblin got control and whooped as he did a U-turn.

"Coming through!" he squealed.

The other goblin howled with laughter as more people tutted and hurried aside. The fairies looped back on themselves, and the long-nosed goblin suddenly whipped his head around.

"I thought I saw something annoying out of the corner of my eye," he yelled. "Fairies! Drive faster and get away from them."

The dodgem car pulled ahead and
swerved past the refreshment stands. The
long-nosed goblin grabbed the wheel
and the goblin with goggles leaned out
towards the stalls. He snatched handfuls
of toffee apples, snow cones and popcorn,

and started hurling them at the fairies. The fairies dodged left and right as the funfair snacks whizzed past their heads.

"We can't get close to them," cried Paloma.

"But we can't give up," said Kirsty.

Just then, the car raced past a water-pistol stall, where players were supposed to hit targets with the water pistols. Rachel stopped so suddenly that Paloma and Kirsty bumped into her.

"Paloma, can you magic us back to our normal size?" said Rachel. "Those water pistols have given me an idea."

The fairies swooped down to hide under the water-pistol stall. There, Paloma waved her wand and the girls were human-sized again.

"Now we need a pair of water pistols,"

said Rachel. "Maybe we could borrow some from the stall."

"No need," said Paloma.

She tapped Rachel's hand with her wand, and Rachel found that she was holding a large water pistol. Then the

fairy did the same to Kirsty.

"We have to stop the goblins somehow," said Rachel. "Maybe a squirt of water will do it."

Paloma hid in Rachel's pocket, and the girls ran across to the other side of the funfair. The dodgem car was bumping around stalls, crashing from one ride to another, and being a terrible nuisance. As the goblins zoomed around a corner,

Rachel and Kirsty jumped out and started shooting jets of water.

The long-nosed goblin slammed his enormous foot on the brake.

"Who's doing that?" he squawked.

The girls squirted the water pistols again, and the goblin with goggles sat bolt upright and glared at them.

"Stop it!" he screeched. "You're making me all soggy."

"We'll keep squirting them with water," said Kirsty. "Paloma, while they're shouting, see if you can dive into the dodgem car and find your key ring."

As the goblins squealed at Rachel and Kirsty, Paloma sped out of Rachel's pocket. She flew towards the car, and then there was a bright flash of blue lightning.

The goblins and the dodgem car disappeared!

Frost Fair

"Oh no," cried Rachel, hurrying forward.

Paloma darted into her pocket and the girls looked around, their hearts thumping.

"Someone must have seen that," said

Kirsty with a groan.

They had always kept the magical secrets of the fairies. Had the goblins just given everything away?

"I can't see anyone looking this way," said Rachel.

"Everyone was running away from the dodgem car," Kirsty realised. "No one saw it disappear."

"Thank goodness," said Paloma. "Now we have to work out where they went."

"I think I can guess," said Kirsty. "They must have gone back to Fairyland, to the Ice Castle."

"Then we must follow them," said Paloma. "Find a place to hide, and I will take you to Fairyland."

People were coming back to gather around the stalls again, and helping to clear up the mess that the goblins had made. The girls could hear them talking about the naughty children who had messed around with a dodgem car.

"Thank goodness they didn't see the car disappearing," said Rachel. "Let's duck behind the test-your-strength

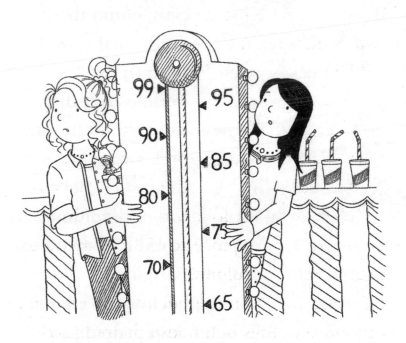

machine."

As soon as they were out of sight,
Paloma fluttered out of Rachel's pocket
and waved her wand. A ribbon as pink
as candyfloss coiled from the tip of her
wand. It wound
itself around the
girls, lifting them
up as they shrank
to fairy size.
Feeling as if they
were sitting in soft,
pink swing boats,
they were rocked
out of the human
world and away to
Fairyland.

The pink ribbon
disappeared, and

Rachel and Kirsty shivered. They had
been transformed into fairies again,
and they were standing in the freezing
grounds of Jack Frost's Castle. Paloma's
wand touched their shoulders, and they
felt fluffy little jackets slip around them.

"I have never seen Jack Frost's castle

grounds look like this before," said Kirsty.

The usual frost-tipped grass and icy hedges had vanished. They were hidden under a vast, Jack Frost-themed funfair. His face decorated the side of the big wheel. Giant Jack Frost soft toys dangled from the coconut shy as prizes. A blue helter-skelter towered above everything, with the top of the slide painted like Jack Frost's open mouth. Sticks of rock were printed with his name, and the candyfloss was bright blue. The funfair stretched from the grim walls of the castle to the edges of the forest, and the fairies shivered.

"He has really done it," said Paloma, shaking her head. "He has built his own funfair."

"But there's hardly anyone here to enjoy it," said Rachel.

The funfair was almost deserted, with only a few goblins dotted here and there.

"It looks more scary than fun to me," said Paloma. "Perhaps the goblins feel the same way."

Just then, the fairies heard giggles echoing from the frozen pond.

"It's the goblins

from the Tippington funfair," said Kirsty.

The goblins were skidding around on the frozen pond in their stolen dodgem car. There were more dodgem cars parked at the edge of the ice, all icy blue.

"They're using the pond as their dodgem rink," said Paloma.

"Those two goblins still have your key ring," said Rachel. "If only there was a way to make them let go of it, even for a moment."

Kirsty looked around, trying to think

of a plan. Then a dazzling
flash of blue caught her
eye.

"Look," she said in a
low voice. "Up there!"

The Ice Lord was
standing at the top
of the helter-skelter.
The cold wind
made his cloak
flap behind him,

and his eyes glittered as he glared at Kirsty.

"I've got a plan," Kirsty said. "Follow me."

The fairies fluttered into the air and zoomed towards the helter-skelter. Jack Frost watched them coming. His face twisted into a mocking smile.

"Come to find some real fun at my amazing funfair?" he sneered. "Sorry, bad luck, no fairies allowed!"

He threw back his head and cackled with laughter. His spiky beard glittered like the icicles that hung from the battlements.

"We're here to get Paloma's magical key ring back," said Rachel, hovering in front of Jack Frost.

He shrugged his shoulders and folded his arms.

"You can't have it," he replied. "You've stolen the first two key rings I had. I need this one to make my funfair brilliant."

"If your funfair is that good, shouldn't you be down there enjoying it?" Paloma asked.

"It *is* that good," Jack Frost bellowed. "It's the best and biggest funfair in the world. That's why I'm standing up here to admire it."

"Funfairs aren't supposed to be stared at," said Kirsty. "They're supposed to be enjoyed. Look at those goblins in the dodgem car."

Jack Frost peered down at the goblins, who were spinning around the frozen pond, shrieking with laughter.

"That does look like fun," he said, narrowing his eyes. "So why are those goblins enjoying something that belongs to me?"

The Snow Car

He gathered up his flapping cloak and sprang on to one of the thick helter-skelter mats. Whooping and cackling, he whizzed down and out of sight.

The fairies flew down and watched Jack Frost shoot off the bottom of the helter-skelter. His mat bounced on the hard ground three times before stopping next to the pond.

"Ouch!" he yelled.

He jumped to his feet and marched to the edge of the pond, rubbing his bottom.

"Stop!" he hollered at the goblins.

At once, the goblins slammed on the brakes. The dodgem stayed in the middle

of the ice, spinning slowly
on the spot. The goblins
stared at Jack Frost in
terror. He stepped on
to the ice and walked
towards them.

"Hand over that
magical key ring," he
hissed. "You've had way
too much fun in that
dodgem car. Too much fun
isn't good for goblins. It's my turn now."

The fairies were now hovering above
him, watching every move he made. He
neared the side of the car and held out
his hand.

"Key ring!" he demanded.

The long-nosed goblin held out his fist
and slowly uncurled his fingers. On his

green palm was a golden key ring. Jack Frost's bony fingers reached out towards it. He was almost there.

WHOOSH! Rachel swooped down and made a grab for the key ring.

"No!" squealed the goblin with goggles.

He leapt up, knocking the other goblin's arm upwards. The key ring spun into the

air and fell on to the ice.

"No!" shouted Jack Frost as the key ring slid across the ice.

"Paloma!" Rachel cried.

All the fairies dived towards the key ring, but Jack Frost flung himself across the ice on his belly. He scooped the key ring up, twisted his body around and sprang up into the air like a jack-in-the-box. He landed next to the dodgem car and smirked at the fairies.

"That's how it's done," he crowed.

Rachel felt her heart sink, and Kirsty bit her lip.

"Maybe we'll never get my magical key ring back," said Paloma in a tiny voice.

Jack Frost cackled in triumph and climbed into the dodgem car, flicking his cloak out behind him.

"Now I'm going to have some fun," he said.

Clutching the key ring in his hand, Jack Frost pointed straight at the other dodgem cars that were parked at the edge of the pond. His dodgem car started to move towards them, faster and faster, until it bumped into them with a loud crash. The other cars skidded sideways, and Jack Frost chased them, bumping

them again and again.

"This is the best ride anywhere ever," he cried. "It's the best funfair anywhere ever. I'm a genius."

A few other goblins had gathered at the edge of the pond, watching Jack Frost with eager eyes.

"Can we have a turn next?" one of them called out.

"No," Jack Frost snarled. "It's mine, all mine! I'm staying in here all day, do you hear me?"

"Wow, he really loves crashing those dodgems," said Rachel.

"That gives me another idea," said Kirsty suddenly.

She whispered in Paloma's ear, and the Dodgems Fairy smiled. Then she raised her wand. The nearby trees shook themselves, sending piles of soft, fluffy snow flying through the air towards the fairies. As the snow reached Paloma, she used her wand to shape it, like an artist using a paintbrush. Seconds later, a perfect dodgem car, made out of snow, was standing on the ice beside her.

"Now we just have to hope that Jack Frost tries to bump into it," said Kirsty, crossing her fingers.

When Jack Frost saw the giant dodgem car, a mean grin spread over his face.

"Something else to ram and slam," he said, cackling.

He spun his steering wheel and zoomed towards the snowy dodgem car. FLUMP! He hit it as hard as he could.

Back to Tippington

Snow exploded around Jack Frost, and the dodgem car spun wildly. In the confusion, he let go of the key ring, and it went flying into the air.

"No!" he yelled.

He rubbed the snow out of his eyes just in time to see the key ring land safely

in Rachel's outstretched hand. Beaming
with happiness, Paloma took her magical
key ring from Rachel.

"I've hardly let myself hope that I
would get this back," she said, clasping it
to her chest. "Thank you both with all

my heart. Now I
can help to keep
funfairs fun for
everyone."

Jack Frost
clambered out
of the dodgem
car, looking like
a slightly spiky
snowman.

"Get this snow
off me," he roared
at the goblins on
the edge of the pond. "Don't just stand
there gawping at me like guppies. Move!"

The goblins stepped on to the ice and
slipped, staggered and scrabbled their way
over to the Ice Lord. They were trying
to keep straight faces, but little blasts of

laughter kept escaping from them. All
that could be seen of Jack Frost were his
furious eyes.

"I'm waiting," he yelled.

Still sniggering, the goblins reached him
and started to brush the snow off. Paloma
flew over to speak to him, and Rachel
and Kirsty followed her.

"Funfairs are meant to be fun for everyone," said Paloma, hovering in front of Jack Frost. "I wish that you could see how much more fun you would have if you shared."

"Sharing isn't fun, you foolish flapping fairy," snapped Jack Frost, pulling off one of his boots and emptying snow out of it. "I'm better and more important than everyone else, so why should I share?"

"It's not nice to keep things to yourself," said Kirsty. "Part of the fun is seeing your friends laughing and enjoying the same things as you."

"What a load of codswallop," Jack Frost muttered, shaking snow out of his sleeve.

"It's time for us to go," said Paloma.

"Good riddance," said Jack Frost. "And there's no need for you to look so happy. I've still got the last magical key ring, and I'm going to make sure that you never get it back."

"You won't succeed," said Rachel. "Friendship and happiness will always win in the end."

Jack Frost stuck out his tongue as Paloma

waved her wand. The girls were whisked up in a starry whirlwind and whooshed back to the human world. Feeling a little breathless, they found themselves standing behind the test-your-strength machine. Their fluffy jackets had disappeared. Paloma gave each of them a delicate kiss on the cheek.

"I'm going straight to the Fairyland funfair," she said, her cheeks pink with excitement. "I can't wait to tell the other Funfair Fairies that we did it."

"Please tell Bobbi that we're ready to help her whenever she needs us," said Kirsty.

"I will," Paloma promised. "Goodbye, and thank you!"

She tapped her wand against her toes and disappeared feet first, leaving a trace of sparkling fairy dust in the air. Rachel grabbed Kirsty's hand.

"Come on," she said. "Let's go and see if the dodgem rink is mended."

They were only a few steps away from the test-your-strength machine when they saw Matilda and Georgia running over to them.

"The dodgems are working again," Georgia called out.

The twins took their hands, and together they all started to hurry towards the dodgem rink.

"It's the weirdest thing," said Matilda. "One minute the dodgems had no power, all except for one car that flew off the rink and skidded around the funfair. Then suddenly the dodgems started working perfectly again."

"Someone even managed to get the missing car back on the rink," Georgia added. "But you'll never guess what we found on the seat. Snow!"

"Weird things often happen at funfairs," said Matilda. "That's part of what makes them such exciting places. Mum and Dad said they have no idea what was wrong with the dodgems. They just started working again. It was like magic."

The four girls joined the queue for the dodgems, and Rachel and Kirsty exchanged a secret smile. Matilda and Georgia would be astonished to find out that it really had been magic! They watched the dodgem cars whizzing around the rink, filled with squealing,

giggling children.

"It's our turn," said Kirsty when the dodgems slowed down and slid to a halt.

Kirsty and Rachel chose a gold car, and Matilda and Georgia climbed into a silver one.

"Get ready ..." called Becky. "Go!"

Rachel and Kirsty shared the steering as they whizzed around the rink, trying to bump the other cars out of their way. Some bumps were so hard that they were lifted off their seats, their hair flying around their heads. Soon they were laughing so hard that it was difficult to catch their breath. The coloured lights

flashed and the music blared out. For a few minutes they forgot everything in the sheer joy of driving the dodgem car.

At last the music died down and the dodgems stopped. Dizzy and giggly, the girls clung to each other as they climbed out of the car and staggered off the rink.

"I hope that the Summer Fair in Fairyland will be that much fun when it opens tonight," said Kirsty.

"It'll be spectacular," said Rachel. "As long as we can find the last magical key ring."

"We will," said Kirsty. "The Funfair Fairies are depending on us, and so are the queen and king. We just have to wait to hear from Bobbi."

"In the meantime, let's enjoy the funfair," said Rachel, seeing Matilda and

Georgia dashing over to them. "Watching
Jack Frost on his helter-skelter really
made me want to go on one too."

"Did someone say 'helter-skelter'?" said
Matilda with a grin.

"We'll race you," said Kirsty, smiling back at Matilda. "Last one to the top buys the toffee apples!"

The End

Now it's time for Kirsty and
Rachel to help...

Bobbi the Bouncy Castle Fairy

Read on for a sneak peek...

"Helter-skelter, toffee apples, toasted
sandwiches, merry-go-round, big wheel,"
said Kirsty Tate, checking each thing off
on her fingers. "It's been a super morning.
What shall we do next?"

She was lying in the grass, side by side
with her best friend, Rachel Walker.
They were on the playing field of
Rachel's school in Tippington, where The
Fernandos' Fabulous Funfair was in full
swing. Matilda and Georgia Fernando
came to join them.

"Would you like to go on the bouncy
castle?" Georgia asked.

Rachel and Kirsty had met the
Fernando twins the day before. Their
parents ran the funfair, and all four girls
had been enjoying it together.

"That's a great idea," said Rachel,
sitting up at once.

"How about a bouncing competition?"
said Matilda. "Let's see who can bounce
the highest."

The girls scrambled to their feet and
linked arms.

"Thank you for inviting me to stay
with you this weekend," Kirsty said
to Rachel as they walked towards the
woods at the edge of the school playing
field.

"I couldn't enjoy it as much if you
weren't here," said Rachel, smiling at her.

Georgia pointed to some trees ahead.

"The bouncy castle is just over there,"

she said.

"Those children must have just been bouncing on it," said Matilda.

A crowd of children was walking towards them. But as they got closer, the girls saw that the children looked very unhappy.

"I can't believe it," Rachel heard one of the boys say in a disappointed voice. "What's a funfair without a bouncy castle?"

"That doesn't sound very good," said Rachel.

The girls started to run, and they soon reached the place where the bouncy castle was supposed to be. They stopped and stared at a huge heap of crumpled-up purple plastic. The castle was deflated.

"No one could bounce on this," said Georgia with a groan. "No wonder those children were disappointed."

"We'd better go and tell Mum and Dad," said Matilda. "Hopefully they'll be able to sort it out. We'll catch up with you later on."

Matilda and Georgia hurried away. Rachel looked down and let out a cry of surprise.

"Look there," she said. "Under one of the castle turrets."

Read **Bobbi the Bouncy Castle Fairy** to find out what adventures are in store for Kirsty and Rachel!

Calling all parents, carers and teachers!
The Rainbow Magic fairies are here to help
your child enter the magical world of reading.
Whatever reading stage they are at, there's
a Rainbow Magic book for everyone!
Here is Lydia the Reading Fairy's guide to
supporting your child's journey at all levels.

1

Starting Out
Our Rainbow Magic Beginner Readers are perfect for first-time readers who are just beginning to develop reading skills and confidence. Approved by teachers, they contain a full range of educational levelling, as well as lively full-colour illustrations.

2

Developing Readers
Rainbow Magic Early Readers contain longer stories and wider vocabulary for building stamina and growing confidence. These are adaptations of our most popular Rainbow Magic stories, specially developed for younger readers in conjunction with an Early Years reading consultant, with full-colour illustrations.

3

Going Solo
The Rainbow Magic chapter books – a mixture of series and one-off specials – contain accessible writing to encourage your child to venture into reading independently. These highly collectible and much-loved magical stories inspire a love of reading to last a lifetime.

www.rainbowmagicbooks.co.uk

"Rainbow Magic got my daughter reading chapter books. Great sparkly covers, cute fairies and traditional stories full of magic that she found impossible to put down" - Mother of Edie (6 years)

"Florence LOVES the Rainbow Magic books. She really enjoys reading now" - Mother of Florence (6 years)

The Rainbow Magic Reading Challenge

Well done, fairy friend – you have completed the book!
This book was worth 5 points.

See how far you have climbed on the
Reading Rainbow opposite.

The more books you read, the more points you will get,
and the closer you will be to becoming a Fairy Princess!

How to get your Reading Rainbow
1. Cut out the coin below
2. Go to the Rainbow Magic website
3. Download and print out your poster
4. Add your coin and climb up the Reading Rainbow!

There's all this and lots more at
www.rainbowmagicbooks.co.uk

You'll find activities, competitions, stories, a special
newsletter and complete profiles of all the
Rainbow Magic fairies. Find a fairy with your name!